THE LOST HEART

Written By
Clare Anderson & Sim Crowther

THE LOST HEART STONE

Printed in the UK by Banbury Litho
First Published March 2023

ISBN: 9781912494491

www.sensoryretreats.com
www.elflanduk.com

This Book Belongs to:

_____

For Rory
Always in my thoughts and a constant source of comfort
and guidance from afar.

"Magic is believing in yourself. If you can do that, you can
make anything happen."
- Goethe

Free Audio Book

THE LOST HEART STONE

Scan this QR code for the FREE
audio book read by co-author, Sim Crowther.

Also included at the end of the story is a QR Code to download
a guided Sleepy Elf Visualisation to help you relax and sleep.

I bet you didn't know that Dragons hatch from eggs! Did you?

Well, when a dragon has hatched and you look inside the shell, you will always find a rose-coloured stone made of quartz. This is the baby dragon's magical Heart Stone. This special quartz stone helps a young dragon feel happy and brave and enables them to make friends.

Because of the Heart Stone, all baby dragons are friendly and cuddly when they are born. Friendly cuddles help them grow big and strong. Rose-coloured quartz is very pretty. For thousands of years, some people have believed that quartz crystals have special powers.

Rose-coloured quartz is thought to grow feelings of love, trust and harmony and some people think it may even help if you are feeling unwell. It is thought that the soothing colour of the stone and it's smooth touch can help if you want to feel peaceful and calm.

You can see why a Heart Stone like this would be so precious to a baby dragon!

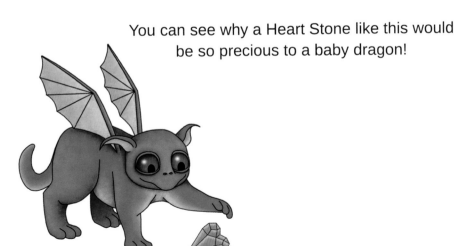

Meet the characters

Baby Gizmo

A baby dragon with a strong sense of right and wrong, Gizmo is bright and inquisitive, and he loves to make friends.

Nibbles

Imaginative and playful, Nibbles doesn't always make good choices but he's full of fun and loved by all.

Rory

Kind and giving, Rory looks after all the wishes of the woodland creatures and helps them come true.

Jessie

A bouncy rabbit with limitless energy
and a thirst for adventure. She's never
still for long!

Autumn

A calm and creative woodland elf,
Autumn is in tune with nature and
a great problem-solver.

Annie

A friendly young dragon with a heart
of gold, Annie is often brave and
always ready to help others.

Remi

A gentle and magical elf, Remi's
comforting presence and soothing voice
helps children everywhere rest,
relax and sleep.

Gizmo the dragon was lonely one day,
He had no friends to ask over to play.
"Be quiet and be still!" his mummy had said,
"And stay near the cave or you'll go straight to bed."

"And don't touch that heart stone!" she called as she flew,
Away from the cave, for she had stuff to do.
Well Gizmo was good… most of the time,
But couldn't remember his mummy's last line.

He didn't have friends to entertain him,
And without any toys, his morning looked grim.
Then Gizmo remembered the heart stone he had.
He went to fetch it. That couldn't be bad.

A heart stone is magic and makes dragons happy,
It helps them make friends and it makes them less snappy.
But Gizmo was bored so he started to roll,
It all round the clearing and into a goal.

Up in a tree there, a squirrel we spy!
His name is Nibbles, he's hidden up high.
He wanted to play but he was a bit cheeky,
So he watched and he waited and acted all sneaky.

Nibbles loved games and he wanted to laugh,
But it's not always easy to know how to ask,
If you can join in to have fun with another.
Nibbles did not have a sister or brother.

Oh no! What's this? Gizmo's rolled it too hard,
The stone's zipped away but it can't have gone far.
Nibbles can see it. He's quick as a flash,
He scoops up the heart stone, runs off at a dash.

"That's mine!" Gizmo shouts. "You rascal! Come back!"
But Nibbles is off and he flies down the track.
The dragon gives chase but he's soon out of puff,
And he slumps to the ground in a terrible huff.

But then he spots Rory, an elf by the stream,
He's special in Elfland, he looks after dreams.
Gizmo knew Rory helped wishes come true,
Rory's so clever, he'd know what to do!

The Star Wish Elf tells him that he's seen the squirrel,
But all that he left was a very short riddle.
They look at the leaf on which it is printed,
The leaf that was dropped when Nibbles had sprinted.

Gizmo the Dragon, you'll never catch me,

I'm far too smart and fast and free.

But look for me everywhere, high and low,

Maybe you'll find me where flowers grow.

ELfLand
N
W
E
S
Rabbit Warren
Stinky Swamp
Jessie's Burrow
Lavender
Bridge
Astaria Entrance
Enchanted Forest
Gizmo's Cave
Wellness Woods
Rory's House
Autumn's House
Elfland Entrance

Lavender
Lane

"I know where he's going. I have here a map!"
Rory pulled paper from under his cap.
He pointed a finger at Lavender Lane.
"That's where he's off to. I know his game."

Rory spoke kindly for Gizmo looked sad.
"I'll help you find him and then you'll feel glad."
"Thanks!" exclaimed Gizmo. "But, are you sure?"
"Think nothing of it. It's what friends are for."

The duo set off in pursuit of the thief,
They hurried along and the journey was brief.
They soon arrived breathless on Lavender Lane,
And saw something there that was hard to explain.

Out of the blooms, sprang a big fluffy ball,
It bounced and it flipped, and it dizzied them all.
It suddenly stopped and they saw it had paws,
"A rabbit!" they said with a round of applause.

"Ah Jessie," said Rory, "we're looking for Nibbles.
You know the one, he's that sneaky squirrel."
"He's taken my heart stone," said Gizmo quite sadly,
"For me to be happy, I need it quite badly."

Jessie thought for a moment, then bounced as she said,
"I have seen a squirrel. He dropped this as he fled."
She held out a leaf, all scrumpled and green,
On it, some words could be easily seen.

Gizmo the Dragon, you'll never catch me,

I'm far too smart and fast and free.

This game makes me thirsty. What do you think?

Find me somewhere we can all have a drink.

Berry Café

"I know where he's gone!" Cried Jessie with glee,
"All gather round and listen to me.
The Berry Café is where we must go,
Everyone goes there for fruit drinks you know!"

Jessie spoke kindly for Gizmo looked sad.
"I'll help you find him and then you'll feel glad."
"Thanks!" exclaimed Gizmo. "But, are you sure?"
"Think nothing of it. It's what friends are for."

So off they all went to the Berry Café,
To find Gizmo's heart stone and save the day.
Rory was leading and holding the map,
A miserable Gizmo just trailed at the back.

They walked and they bounced and they finally made it,
Just in time, for their hopes almost faded.
The Café was busy. The fruit snacks were good,
The best spot to eat in the Elfland Woods.

Annie, a dragon, was playing outside,
They stopped and they asked if a squirrel she'd spied.
She thought for a moment and then she said "Yes!
Nibbles has been here but how did you guess?"

"He's left us some clues." Rory calmly replied.
"He's stolen my heart stone!" Gizmo angrily cried.
"Now then," said Rory, "that's not quite the case,
I'm sure he's just playing to make us give chase."

"He wasn't here long," Annie said with a smile.
"He dropped this big leaf. It could be worthwhile,
To look at the words that are written just here."
They all gathered round and the riddle was clear.

Gizmo the Dragon, you'll never catch me,

I'm far too smart and fast and free.

I know that you must want your heart stone back,

You just have to look in Autumn's sack.

ELFLand

Stinky Swamp

Rabbit Warren

Jessie's Burrow

Lavender Lane

Believe Bridge

Astaria Entrance

Berry Café

Enchanted Forest

Floating Stepping Stones

Gizmo's Cave

Nibble's Drey

Wellness Woods

Rory's House

Autumn's House

Here be

"I know what this means!" Annie said with a grin.
The others all stood around scratching their chins.
"Autumn the elf is what Nibbles is saying,
Not Autumn the season. Nibbles is playing."

Annie spoke kindly for Gizmo looked sad.
"I'll help you find him and then you'll feel glad."
"Thanks!" exclaimed Gizmo. "But, are you sure?"
"Think nothing of it. It's what friends are for."

They set off once more through the beautiful wood,
To find Gizmo's heart stone and make him feel good.
Rory was leading and holding the map,
A miserable Gizmo just trailed at the back.

The trees began changing, the leaves turning red,
Then Jessie spied Autumn there, just up ahead.
Autumn was scooping some leaves in a sack,
She looked as the others approached down the track.

"Hi Autumn!" called Rory and gave her a grin,
"We're looking for Nibbles but haven't seen him."
"I have," said Autumn, "he raced past me here,
He had a pink heart stone and seemed in good cheer."

"He threw a green leaf in my sack here you see?
But ran off again without talking to me."
"That must be the clue but that hardly seems fair,"
Said Annie, "for no one will find it in there!"

Well Jessie was quick and she dived in the sack,
She rustled and rummaged. The others stood back.
Then, out shot the rabbit all squeaky with glee,
Holding one leaf that they all had to see.

Gizmo the Dragon, you'll never catch me,

I'm far too smart and fast and free.

But Gizmo, I just want to be your friend,

So where we began is now the end.

ELfLand

N
W   E
S

Rabbit Warren

Stinky Swamp

Jessie's Burrow

Lavender Lane

Believe Bridge

Astaria Entrance

Berry Café

Floating Stepping Stones

Enchanted Forest

Nibble's Drey

Wellness Woods

Annie's Cave

Autumn's House

Here be dragons!

Gizmo's Cave

"That doesn't make sense," Gizmo said with a groan,
"How will I ever get back my heart stone?"
But Autumn was clever and had a brainwave,
"I think what he means is get back to the cave."

Autumn spoke kindly for Gizmo looked sad.
"I'll help you find him and then you'll feel glad."
"Thanks!" exclaimed Gizmo. "But, are you sure?"
"Think nothing of it. It's what friends are for."

They set off again on the big squirrel hunt,
But Gizmo was worried and ran on in front.
Soon they were back where the game had begun,
The others found Gizmo alone looking glum.

"There's nobody here and my heart stone is gone.
He thinks it's a game but the game is all wrong.
And now I'll be lonely and mum will be cross."
The others looked sad, they were all at a loss.

But Rory was wise and said "Gizmo just look!
You made all these friends when your heart stone he took."
Everyone smiled in that kind little huddle,
Then they wrapped Gizmo up in a nice cosy cuddle.

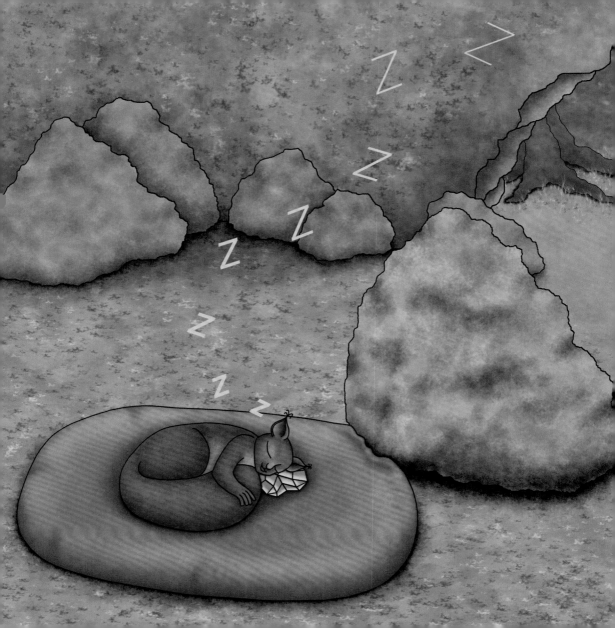

"But where is my heart stone I wonder?" He cried,
"Mum still won't be pleased." Gizmo said with a sigh.
Autumn was looking for clues on the ground,
"Aha!" she said loudly. What had she found?

Some footprints were leading direct to the cave,
Together the friends were determined and brave.
They crept to the cave to begin some exploring,
And there they found Nibbles sleeping and snoring.

He was curled up and comfy on Gizmo's soft bed.
The heart stone was there right under his head.
Jessie nudged Nibbles, who stirred and woke up.
"Oh. Hi everybody", yawned Nibbles, "Whassup?"

"Nibbles," said Rory, "you need to say sorry.
Gizmo, my friend, has been ever so worried.
You took his heart stone and wanted to play,
But you should have asked him. What do you say?

We've had fun with your game and we don't feel too bad,
But that stone is precious and Gizmo was sad."
"Sorry," said Nibbles, "I just wanted a friend,
I didn't imagine how this would all end."

"OK," Gizmo said with a smile and a shrug,
He stepped up to Nibbles and gave him a hug.
"My heart stone is safe so there's no real harm done,
I loved all your clues and your game was quite fun."

"Oh great!" Nibbles cried, "Shall we play a bit more?"
The others cried, "NOOOOOO!" And they slumped to the floor.
"I think," Rory said, "that we're all a bit jaded."
The squirrel looked down and his happiness faded.

"Don't worry," said Gizmo, "we'll play again soon,
Perhaps by the light of tonight's Luna moon?
For now, a nice sleep would be good for our health."
"Quite right," agreed Rory, "I know just the elf!"

The others all waved. "Bye for now!" the friends said,
Then Rory tucked Gizmo snug into his bed.
He murmured some magic and who should arrive,
The Sleepy Elf, Remi to help them revive.

She was an expert and knew what was best,
For tired little dragons who needed a rest.
She spoke of a forest and bubbling stream,
Soon Gizmo was sleepy and ready to dream.

"Thank you for helping me find my heart stone,"
sighed Gizmo to Rory, "I'm glad to be home."
"Friends help each other," said Rory, "I'm sure.
You're my friend Gizmo, It's what friends are for."

Thank you for reading.
We hope you enjoyed our rhyming adventure.

Now you have finished the story, here is
a special treat to help you sleep...

A Guided Sleepy Elf Visualisation .

Just scan the QR code and press play.

Meet the Creators of The Lost Heart Stone

Sim Crowther   **Siena Brooke**   **Natalie Samuel**   **Clare Anderson**

We want all children to enjoy wonderful bedtime reading experiences that not only entertain and inspire the imagination, but also provide the comfort and calm that is so important for deep relaxation and restful sleep.

To achieve this, award-winning beauty entrepreneur and founder of Sensory Retreats, Clare Anderson assembled a "dream team" that includes author and former primary school teacher, Sim Crowther and qualified psychotherapist, hypnotherapist and holistic wellbeing practitioner, Natalie Samuel.

The Elfland book series is the creative vision of Clare and her young daughter Siena. Their bedtime discussions lead to a magical imaginary world filled with fascinating characters and they have, so far, inspired two books and a range of wellbeing products and ideas for younger children including Dreamy Eyes and Elf Eyes self-heating eye masks and cuddly toys.

Together, the Elfland book team are devoted to creating exciting, adventure stories with gentle wellbeing messages and themes of friendship and kindness woven throughout. With beautiful illustrations by Emma Kurran, they're designed to be interactive and engaging.

The Lost Heart Stone is brought to life by a free audio version which is voiced by co-author, Sim. Complementing each book in the series is a Guided 'Sleepy Elf' Visualisation, devised and narrated by Natalie, to settle and calm the listener and promote good quality sleep. Within the book, you will also find a selection of read-aloud sayings for children which are intended to grow their self-belief and help to start each new day on a positive note.

THE LOST WISH

Discover the magical story of The Lost Wish for FREE.

The Lost Wish is the 1st book in the Elfland Series

Scan the QR to get the first
30 chapters of the ebook for FREE

To receive the final part of the book for free please email
hello@elflanduk.com

The full ebook and paperback book can be purchased at Amazon,
Elfland UK, Sensory Retreats and leading bookstores.

Positive Sayings

We hope you enjoyed the story of The Lost Heart Stone.
We created the book to make you smile and to show how kindness, friendship and forgiveness are so important for wellbeing. Positive thinking also makes a big difference to how we feel inside and to how we treat others. On the following pages, you will find lots of Elfland characters and their favourite daily sayings. When you say them out loud, after a good night's sleep, they can help you start each new day full of positivity and self-belief.

What will you choose to do today?

Today I will...

Baby Gizmo...speak to someone new and make a friend.

Nibbles...listen to others and understand.

Rory...glow warm and bright like a star.

Jessie...be patient and calm to help others feel safe.

Annie...help my teacher and make them smile.

Autumn...take pride in the fabulous work that I do.

Ginger...not be afraid to ask for help.

Mr White...tell my family how much I love them.

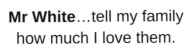

Brooke…share a favourite book with a special friend.

Biscuit…be happy... be bright...be me!

Arthur…practise a skill I find difficult.

Albie…work hard and strive to be the best I can be.

Eve…use my smile to spread a little joy wherever I go.

Noelle…spend time with friends who bring out the best in me.

Buddy…be faithful and true to my friends.

Miss Clarke…create something lovely for a person I care about.

Lester…choose to be happy and spread my joy.

Perrie…sprinkle a little magic over my family and friends.

Eleuia…push myself and reach for the stars.

Bow… puff out my chest and raise my chin.

Mr Connors…set an example of friendship and forgiveness.

Mr Arwin…make an effort to learn something new.

Pretzel…share my wonderful ideas with other people.

Cookie…make something delicious for others to enjoy.

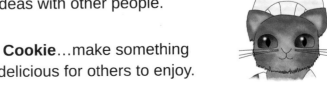